Pranks for Nothing!

Adapted by Jane Mason and Sara Hines Stephens

Based on "Prank Week" written by
Anthony Del Broccolo and
"Webcam" written by Dan Schneider

Based on *Zoey 101* created by Dan Schneider

SCHOLASTIC INC.

New York   Toronto   London   Auckland   Sydney
Mexico City   New Delhi   Hong Kong   Buenos Aires

No part of this publication may be reproduced in whole or in part, stored in a retrieval system, or transmitted in any form or by any means, electronic, mechanical, photocopying, recording, or otherwise, without written permission of the publisher. For information regarding permission, write to Scholastic Inc., Attention: Permissions Department, 557 Broadway, New York, NY 10012.

ISBN 0-439-83159-8

12 11 10 9 8 7 6 5 4 3 2   6 7 8 9 10/0

Printed in the U.S.A.

First printing, January 2006

Rude Awakening

Zoey Brooks rolled over in her cozy bed just as her digital clock clicked from 6:59 to 7:00 a.m. A smooth groove played softly, and Zoey slowly opened one eye. It was time to get up.

With a big stretch, Zoey sat up and pushed her blue striped comforter back. "Wake up, guys. It's seven." She wished she and her roommates could all lounge around for a while, but they had to get ready and get to class. The academics at Pacific Coast Academy — their new boarding school — were serious business. The teachers did *not* like tardiness.

Dana Cruz rolled over with a stretch and a yawn. "I'm up," she said sleepily. Dana was not exactly known as an early riser. Zoey had to hand it to her, though: She'd been doing a great job adjusting to their grueling school schedule.

Zoey's gaze moved from Dana's lower bunk to Nicole Bristow's top one. It was empty. "Where's Nicole?" she asked. The perkier of her two roommates, Nicole was often the first one out of bed. But she always woke Zoey before she left the room to take her morning shower.

"Up there," Dana said. She lay back down and kicked the mattress above her. "Nicole, wake up," she said.

Zoey shook her head. "She isn't up there. Where could she be?"

Suddenly the covers right next to her moved, and Nicole appeared in her purple jammies with her pink stuffed teddy bear. "Hi," she said cheerfully.

Zoey screamed and fell to the floor with a thud. Sitting up, she stared at her friend. What the heck was she doing in her bed? "Nicole, what are you doing?" Zoey asked, a little exasperated. This had better be good.

"I had a bad dream in the middle of the night," Nicole said with a shrug. "Usually when I have a bad dream, I crawl in bed with my mom, but she's back home in Kansas." She eyed Zoey a little sheepishly. "Did I scare you?"

Zoey rolled her eyes. Nicole was a great friend, but was she kidding? "Oh, no. I always wake up with a scream and a quick heart attack," she said sarcastically.

Nicole looked apologetic. "I'm sorry," she said. Crawling into bed with Zoey had seemed like a good idea at four o'clock in the morning.

Just then, there was a loud pounding on the door. "Quick!" a familiar voice called. It was Quinn, the dorm's resident science freak. She was totally strange, but nice in a geeky sort of way. "Come outside! You gotta see this!"

Suddenly Quinn was whisked away with the throng of girls running down the hall. Something was definitely up.

Zoey gave her roommates a confused look and ran out with everyone else. Dana and Nicole were right on her heels. When they got outside, Zoey blinked. Then her eyes adjusted to the morning light and her jaw dropped. Their entire dorm and the surrounding trees were covered with white stuff.

"Somebody TP'd our dorm!" Zoey cried. The stringy sheets of paper were draped off of everything in sight. Gross!

"And there's toilet paper everywhere!" Nicole added, stating the obvious. Zoey and Dana gave her a look. Nicole was great, but sometimes she was a little slow on the uptake.

"Who did this?" Quinn demanded. Dressed in an

orange shirt and blue flannel snowflake bottoms, she stared at the dangling white paper as if it was a science experiment gone wrong.

"That's what *I* wanna know," Dana chimed in, crossing her arms across her green basketball-uniform tank top.

"Wait!" Nicole said cheerfully, still clutching her pink teddy bear. "Maybe this was an accident."

Zoey smiled at her friend. Nicole was always looking on the bright side. But Dana shot her a sideways "get a clue" look.

"This was noooo accident," Vicki, another girl in the dorm, proclaimed. "This was an attack on the girls' dorm."

"Yeah," the girls chorused.

"Yeah, and whoever did it's gonna pay!" Dana vowed, glaring at the paper fluttering from the dorm windows and trees. Dana was tough. Nobody messed with her or her friends.

All around Zoey, the girls began to echo in agreement. This was *not* going to be taken lightly.

"Yeah!" Quinn shouted, flicking a streamer of toilet paper off her shoulder. "We'll hunt them down and surgically remove their kidneys!"

Whoa! The girls were speechless. They stared at Quinn as if she had horns growing out of her head.

Quinn looked around at her female schoolmates. What did she say? "I mean, whoever did this is gonna pay!" she exclaimed, changing her tune and pounding her fist in her hand for emphasis.

Everyone cheered. The girls were in agreement. They would not put up with these shenanigans.

Prank Week

Zoey carried her tray to an empty table and plunked it down. After the TP episode and the long morning of classes, she was ready to have some lunch and hang out with her friends. Pulling her chair back, she felt the ocean breeze on her face. One of the best things about PCA was the weather — and the view! The school was set right on the southern California coast, so the Pacific Ocean provided a shimmering backdrop to the already gorgeous campus filled with lush lawns, gurgling fountains, and modern white buildings.

"Ulch," Dana groaned as she set her tray next to Zoey's. Her hoop earrings bobbed when she shook her head. "I thought that class was never gonna end."

Zoey knew how she felt. The classes at PCA were tough, and sometimes the teachers moved so fast it was practically impossible to keep up. Only in this case, Dana was talking about the opposite problem.

"Why does history have to be so boring?" Zoey asked. She was in full agreement with her roomie on this one.

Nicole pulled her chair out and sat down. "You know why history's boring?" she said, plopping into a chair and pulling off her backpack. "Because none of our past presidents were cute."

Zoey considered this as she popped a grape into her mouth. "Abraham Lincoln was kind of cute," she said thoughtfully.

Dana shot Zoey an "are you kidding?" look. "With that big hat?" she asked.

Nicole nodded emphatically. "Yeah, that big hat kinda killed his cuteness."

Just then, Chase Matthews, Michael Barrett, and Logan Reese set their trays down at the other end of the table.

"What goes on?" Chase greeted them.

"Hey." Logan waved casually.

"What's up?" Michael chimed in, climbing over the back of his chair and pulling off his bike messenger bag as he settled into his seat.

Zoey and the girls waved and said hello. Zoey was always happy to see Chase. He was her first and best guy friend at PCA. They'd met on the very first day of school, and Chase had taken the time to show her around and give her the lowdown on life at her new school. Plus, he made her laugh and was a great listener.

Michael was also a good guy — funny and always willing to help out if he could. Logan, on the other hand, was pretty much a jerk. Actually, he was a total jerk. He thought he was the greatest thing on campus and was always talking about how cool he was.

"So, I heard you girls woke up to a little surprise this morning," Logan said with a smirk.

Zoey eyed Logan. It was just like him to think a stunt like that was funny.

"Yeah," Nicole said, still distressed. "Someone TP'd our whole dorm."

Chase nodded. "We saw," he said.

Michael looked like he was trying not to smile. "Yeah, somebody got you guys good."

Dana's dark eyes narrowed. "And we're gonna find out who," she vowed.

"I already have a few theories," Zoey told her friends. She'd been thinking about it all through history class and couldn't believe she hadn't already told them her ideas. "I think it was either the football team or maybe —"

"It was us," Logan boasted.

The girls didn't hear him.

"I bet it was hippies," Nicole threw out.

"*We* did it," Michael said.

The girls kept talking, not really listening to what the guys were saying.

"I hear that some hippies live on the beach, so maybe they snuck on campus last night and —"

All of a sudden Zoey registered what the guys were saying. "Wait a second," she told Nicole, raising a hand to stop her from going on. She stared across the table at the three guys sitting there. "Did you guys just say that you did it?"

"Yeah," Logan said, leaning back and grinning.

"We did it," Michael crowed and proudly pointed at his chest with both index fingers.

"Surprise," Chase said jokingly. Dressed in a navy-blue button-down shirt, he hardly looked like the prankster he was professing to be.

Zoey threw the closest piece of food she could find at Chase.

"Hey!" Chase protested with a laugh. "Don't be throwing grapes!"

Zoey scowled. Did he really think a grape compared to a dozen rolls of toilet paper? She let another one fly, this time at Michael.

"Why'd you guys TP our dorm?" Nicole asked, as if the reason was more important than their guilt.

Logan smiled yet again. "Because it's Prank Week," he said, as if that explained everything.

"Yeah." Chase nodded.

"Prank Week," Michael repeated.

Zoey tried to stay calm, which wasn't easy. She was pretty annoyed. "Okay, what is Prank Week?" she asked.

Logan shook his brown curls off his forehead haughtily. "Don't girls know anything?" he asked.

Dana glared across the table. Who did this shrimpy kid think he was? "I know how to make you cry," she said through narrowed eyes.

Logan pretended to look worried. "What're you gonna do?" he asked.

Dana glared, pushing a highlighted corkscrew curl off her face.

"All right," Zoey said loudly. She was feeling fed up. She just wanted to get to the bottom of this! "I need somebody to tell me what Prank Week is right now!"

"Okay, look," Chase said, holding up his hands.

"It's a tradition we have here at PCA and it happens one week every year."

"This week," Michael added.

Obviously, Zoey thought.

"Yeah, see, the returning students —"

"That'd be us," Logan interrupted.

"Play pranks on all the new students," Chase finished.

"That'd be you," Logan said, his brown eyes flashing.

"It's sort of like your initiation into PCA," Michael explained.

"It's fun," Logan said.

"For us," Michael put in.

"Yeah, not for you," Chase admitted, eyeing the girls from under his mop of curly brown hair.

Zoey was getting the picture, and she didn't like it much. She exchanged looks with her roommates.

"Are you sure this isn't some excuse for the guys to pick on the girls?" Nicole asked pointedly.

Michael shook his head. "No, we do this every year."

"It just so happens that this is the first year girls are allowed into PCA," Chase explained.

"Which makes you prime targets," Logan pointed out, as if that were necessary.

"Okay, and what do *we* do?" Zoey asked. She was pretty sure she knew the answer, but wanted to hear it just to be sure.

"Nothing." Logan shook his head, smiling smugly.

"Except, y'know, get pranked," Chase finished with a sheepish shrug.

Dana had been listening carefully but was not about to keep quiet now that she had the whole picture. "And we're just supposed to take it?" she asked incredulously. Like the girls would be willing to do *that*. Were the guys stupid enough to think that was possible?

"Hey, they're catchin' on!" Logan quipped.

"Okay, well, I think Prank Week is idiotic," Zoey said. She didn't really see the point of pulling stunts on the new kids. After all, it was hard enough to get used to boarding school — especially one that had only just started to let in girls. (What had taken them so long, anyway?)

"Hey, we had to do it our first year," Michael said.

"Yeah," Chase agreed. "And the pranks were pretty harsh. During my first year, some older kids tied me up in the fountain and turned on the water! I couldn't get out and got soaking wet. Everyone thought it was hysterical!"

"Yeah, well, try being chased by a shark!" Michael said. "I was taking a leisurely swim in the pool when I was suddenly attacked by a giant shark! And I was really far from the edge of the pool! I swam as fast as I could, but the shark kept coming closer and closer and closer. I was sure I was going to get eaten, and then two older guys popped up from underneath a fake shark fin."

Dana looked hard at Michael. If he believed there could be a shark in a swimming pool, he deserved to be pranked! Come on!

"Yeah, I guess they were pretty harsh," Logan agreed, getting an embarrassed look on his usually snide face. "I wasn't too pleased to wake up one morning in the middle of campus surrounded by a laughing crowd — they carried my whole bed onto the lawn!" He ran a hand through his curly hair. "Luckily I look good all the time, even first thing in the morning."

Zoey shook her head as she listened to the prank stories. It all seemed kind of silly.

"Well, we're not going to be such easy targets," Dana said defiantly.

Zoey liked that idea. They would prevent themselves from being pranked by paying close attention to what was going on around them.

Michael gulped down the last of his water. "Hey, Nicole, could you toss this in the trash can behind you?" he asked innocently, handing her the bottle.

"Sure," Nicole replied, pushing her chair back and walking over to the trash can. Just as she dropped the bottle into the can, a PCA student leaped out of it, scattering garbage all over the ground.

"Roooaaarrr!" he bellowed.

Nicole screamed and ran — right past the table and her friends! She was moving so fast her pink scarf was nothing but a flash of color.

Logan nodded with satisfaction. "Ya gotta love Prank Week," he said, collecting high fives.

"Totally," Michael agreed.

Zoey glared at the boys, especially Chase. She expected this kind of stuff from someone like Logan, and maybe even Michael. But Chase was supposed to be her good friend.

As far as Zoey was concerned, Prank Week stunk.

CHAPTER 3
Drenched

Logan, Chase, and Michael strolled back toward their dorm. They had just finished a good game of Frisbee — as a kind of celebration for their successful pranking. Last year, Prank Week had been totally lame. Being the prankee was a definite drag. But now that they were the guys doing the pranking, Prank Week ruled!

As they got close to their dorm, Chase noticed a flurry of activity. Several workers were polishing the golden statue that stood beside the building entrance — the statue of the school's founder. Dean Rivers and his secretary were instructing the workers not to miss a spot.

"Hey, Dean Rivers," Chase said. It was always a good idea to try and stay on the good side of school officials, *especially* the dean.

"Boys." The dean ran his hand down his tan blazer lapel as he greeted them.

"What's going on with the statue?" Logan asked, motioning toward the gilded guy.

"I'm having it cleaned." Dean Rivers nodded matter-of-factly. Then, as if to prove his point, he turned back to the workers. "Don't forget to polish his backside," he instructed. One of the workers rolled his eyes and kept cleaning.

"Why are you having it cleaned?" Logan asked. He had never really paid much attention to the golden dude before. Why, all of a sudden, did the statue need its backside polished?

Dean Rivers rocked back and forth on his heels proudly. "Because," he announced, "tomorrow morning I'm having some photos taken in front of it with Mr. Bradford."

Michael, Chase, and Logan exchanged glances. Logan looked confused. Michael looked impressed. "Mr. Bradford?" he asked. His eyes were wide with disbelief.

"The guy who founded PCA?!" Chase sounded as shocked as Michael. The guy must be like a hundred and fifty years old!

"No, no," Dean Rivers shook his head. *That*

Mr. Bradford has been dead for years. His son is coming here."

Chase nodded, finally getting the picture. Of course it couldn't be *the* Mr. Bradford. He would be as petrified as the statue in front of them.

"You boys live in this dorm?" the dean asked, gazing at the lawns surrounding the building.

"Yes, sir," Chase said.

"We do." Logan nodded.

"Uh-huh," Michael muttered, wondering what was coming next.

"Well, make sure it looks perfect. I don't want any trash or teenage items mucking up the grounds." Dean Rivers waved his hand around as if sweeping away invisible garbage.

"No, sir," Michael agreed.

"No trash," Logan added. Was this guy serious?

"Or teenage items," Chase said, slowly rolling his eyes at the other guys. What the heck were "teenage items," anyway?

Zoey balanced on the back of the sofa in the girls' lounge, listening intently to Vicki's every word. The rest of the girls in the dorm were there, too. They had serious business to discuss. Prank Week business.

"Well, I don't think we should just sit around and take it. I think we should prank the guys back," Vicki said. Her almond-shaped eyes were full of determination.

"Yeah!" the rest of the girls chorused.

Folding her arms over her pink shirt, Zoey frowned. Revenge was not what she had in mind. But it was clearly what everyone else had on *their* minds.

Quinn jumped up and faced the table of girls. "Wait, wait!" she squealed, flapping her arms like a bird. "I have the perfect prank!"

Everyone got quiet, waiting to hear Quinn's plan. Zoey was not sure if they were really curious or really scared. You never knew what Quinn was going to come up with.

Nicole held up her hands. "We're not removing anyone's kidneys," she said, looking a little grossed out.

"No, no." Quinn shook her head in Nicole's direction and everyone breathed a sigh of relief. But Zoey guessed that her next idea would be almost as weird.

"We'll wait until it's dark . . ." Quinn said slowly, building suspense.

"Yeah?" one of the girls prompted.

"Then we sneak up to one of the guys' dorms."

"Okay," Vicki said, starting to feel the excitement in the room. Maybe Quinn was on to something good.

Nicole was practically rubbing her hands together like an evil scientist. "Loving this," she said, waiting to hear more.

"Then" — Quinn's eyes were huge behind her square glasses frames — "we set off a sonic high-frequency device and render all of the boys unconscious!" she squealed, hopping up and down like a demented rabbit.

The excitement died fast and the whole room went quiet. Typical Quinn. All theory and no substance.

"Quinn," Nicole broke it to her, "there's no sonic device that renders people unconscious."

"Oh, really?" Quinn said with her hand on her hip. "Just wait." She turned and huffily marched out of the room.

Off to her lab, no doubt, Zoey thought. She got the heebie-jeebies just thinking about it. She could barely believe she had actually shared a room with Quinn for a few days when she wasn't getting along with Dana and Nicole — and survived! Zoey rolled her eyes and watched Quinn disappear out the door.

"Zoey, how come you're not saying anything?" Nicole asked, interrupting Zoey's thoughts. "You always say things," she pointed out.

"I dunno." Zoey shrugged and stood up. "I just don't think we should sink to their level," she explained.

"What do you mean?" Dana asked.

"Well, I mean, we'll prank them, they'll prank us back." She shrugged again, thinking of the stupid back-and-forth of it all. "What's the point?"

"So we should just sit around and be victims?" Nicole could not believe Zoey thought they should just roll over and take it! Where was her backbone?

"Nooo." Zoey shook her head. Of course not! She was not one to be a sitting duck. "I think we should talk to the guys and tell 'em we don't want to be a part of Prank Week," she said reasonably.

Behind her, Vicki spoke up. "But it's a PCA tradition," she pointed out.

"Yeah, and it used to be a tradition that girls weren't even allowed here, but we changed that," Zoey countered. The girls had made a lot of changes since they'd arrived at PCA, too — some traditions were made to be broken.

Everyone began to nod in agreement. The girls had managed to create some new traditions of their own. Maybe Zoey was right.

Suddenly a scream echoed in the lounge. It was coming from outside.

"Aggggh. Help me!" Whoever was yelling

sounded like he was in total agony. And the voice sounded familiar.

Chase? Zoey jumped up and raced out the door with the rest of the girls behind her.

Their dorm was still coated in TP, but the sidewalk outside the modern white building was empty — for a moment.

"And fire!" a voice yelled from above. Logan! On his command, a dozen guys on the nearby lawn started pummeling the girls with water balloons.

They tried to duck and cover, but it was no use. There were a lot of armed pranksters, and the balloons were coming at them fast and furious. Logan lobbed balloons down from the roof. Michael hid behind the bushes, ducking in and out and repeatedly hitting his targets. Chase and a whole army of PCA guys blocked the girls' escape, bombarding them with the latex-and-water weapons.

Balloon after balloon burst on the screaming girls, soaking their clothes, ruining their hair — and really ticking them off.

When Chase saw that everyone was thoroughly drippy, he called a halt to the assault. "All right! All right! They've had enough," he told the guys.

"Cease fire!" Michael ordered, waving his arms and grinning.

The siege came to an abrupt end. Only the hysterical laughter of the victors and a few soggy chuckles from the girls echoed in its wake.

But some of the girls weren't laughing. "You're all done for!" Dana yelled. She was as furious as she was wet. And everyone knew that a furious Dana was a force to be reckoned with.

"It's okay, Dana." Zoey tried to calm her friend down. "It's just water balloons. It's no big deal," Zoey said, trying to shrug it off.

"Incommmmiiiinnnggg!" Logan's voice sounded far off and slow. The girls turned and looked up. When Dana saw what was about to happen, her mouth dropped open. Nicole's glossed lips formed a perfect O. Even Chase looked dumbfounded as the biggest water balloon anyone had ever seen wobbled straight toward Zoey's head.

SPLASH! Zoey took a direct hit. Water gushed over the top of her head, onto her face, into her eyes and mouth. Her outfit was soaked. Her wet hair was stuck to her cheeks.

On the roof, Logan let out a satisfied guffaw.

Zoey scowled. She was done being reasonable.

Reasonable was nothing but a hazy memory. Prank Week had just taken on a whole new meaning.

"All right," Zoey said, dripping fury and water all over the sidewalk. These were not just water balloons anymore. "This means war."

Operation Revenge

That night in the girls' lounge, an important meeting was held. The whole girls' dorm was there, but five of the girls huddled together looking more like Green Berets than middle schoolers. They were dressed in camouflage fatigues and baseball caps and sported dark smears of makeup under their eyes. They were about to go on their first prank mission.

"Okay, everyone knows the plan, right?" Zoey looked at her friends' nodding, expectant faces. She could tell they were ready. And they looked pretty stylin' in camo, too. "Now, let's make sure we've got everything."

"I got the dress." Vicki held up an unusually large, pink, tie-dyed number.

"I found it in the laundry room," Nicole said proudly.

"I got the paint." Dana lifted a clear satchel filled with all kinds of paints and several brushes.

They had everything they needed. It was payback time! The girls were just getting to their feet when Quinn burst into the room. "I did it!" she squealed, her twisty brown braids bouncing.

"What'd you do?" Zoey asked a little nervously. She eyed Quinn in her pink-and-blue shirt. What could the girl be up to now?

"I built this." Quinn cradled a small black ball in both hands. It looked like something out of a sci-fi movie. "It's a sonic neural neutralizer."

Sighing and shaking her head, Dana waited for the translation. "We don't speak geek," she said with an emphatic eye roll.

"Explain," Zoey said a little less harshly.

"Well," Quinn began. "I just push this button, and the neutralizer emits a high-frequency sound that interferes with human brain waves, causing anyone within one hundred yards to lose consciousness." Her face was lit up like a birthday cake. You'd think she'd just invented the remote control. "Shall we try it on the boys?" she asked with a devilish grin.

Nicole was skeptical. "Quinn, that's not gonna

work," she said, shaking her head and causing her ponytail to bob.

Quinn's face fell. "Then you force me to demonstrate!" She held up the device, her finger hovering over the button that activated it. "Prepare to be knocked out!"

The moment Quinn pressed the button, an awful, high-pitched squeal filled the air, and the hands of every girl in the room flew to their ears. They tried to block out the painful noise, but it was impossible. The sound was so piercing, it shattered Quinn's glasses!

"Quinn, turn that off," Zoey shouted. She hoped the girl could hear her over the din. If Quinn did not shut that ball off soon, her eardrums were going to burst.

Behind her cracked lenses, Quinn looked baffled. She deactivated the ball and looked at the roomful of girls glaring at her. "We should all be unconscious. Do you feel dizzy? Confused? Woozy?" she questioned.

"No!" Nicole said, trying to restrain her anger.

"Just annoyed," Zoey said pointedly.

Quinn looked at her invention, perplexed. "It must need some adjustments." She shrugged.

"So must your head," Dana muttered as Quinn turned to go. That girl was the weirdest.

"All right." Zoey had to get her crack prank team back on track. "Let's get this done."

The girls huddled like a basketball team, laying their open hands on top of one another. "Break!" they yelled. They turned to run out of the dorm, totally psyched up — and ran right into their dorm advisor, Coco.

Coco was carrying a large laundry basket and looked cranky, as usual. "Where are you going?" she asked, suspiciously eyeing the girls' outfits.

"Oh, hi, Coco," Nicole said, trying to act casual. She wished they weren't all dressed in camo!

Zoey had to think fast. "Uh, we were just getting ready to study together. The other girls nodded in agreement. Zoey hoped Coco wouldn't notice that none of them had a book or a laptop or even a pencil on them.

"Dressed in camouflage?" Coco asked skeptically.

Zoey looked at Dana, Vicki, and Nicole. They looked as worried as she felt. They were this close to being busted. . . .

"It's a fashion thing," Nicole said.

"Yeah." Zoey was grateful for Nicole's quick thinking. "Camouflage is the new black." She said it like Coco should already know.

"Yeah," the girls echoed.

Coco still looked suspicious. "I see." She looked them all up and down again, then shrugged. "All right. I'm gonna go watch TV."

Breathing silent sighs of relief, the camo team headed for the door.

"Oh, wait!" Coco called them back.

The girls all stopped, dreading to hear what was next. Zoey held her breath.

"Anybody seen any of my clothes in the laundry room? I'm missing some stuff."

Making sure Vicki had her bag hidden behind her back, Zoey and the girls denied everything and dashed into the cool night air to take their revenge.

Backfire

"I can't believe it!" The next morning, Chase stood in front of his dorm shaking his head at the freaky sight he saw before him. He should have been mad, but he could not wipe the smile off his face. When was he going to learn not to underestimate the girls at PCA?

"They're not supposed to prank us back!" Logan said angrily. He could not believe what he was seeing. "That's against PCA tradition!"

"Yeah," Michael agreed, tapping a finger on his chin as he eyed the statue. "But he does look kinda cute."

The gilded statue of Clarence T. Bradford, the founding father of Pacific Coast Academy, had undergone an extreme makeover. He was sporting a pink tie-dyed dress, a wig, and full makeup. He even had ribbons in his curly new hair. Every boy in the quad stopped to stare — they couldn't get over the new look.

"Mornin', boys," Zoey called casually as she walked past the boys' dorm on her way to class with a bunch of her dorm mates.

"Hey, nice statue!" Nicole called, pretending she was just noticing it for the first time.

"It really makes your dorm look special," Dana said, holding back a laugh. The look on Logan's face, in particular, was priceless.

"Hey, Logan, is that your dress on him?" Zoey asked. That did it. The girls cracked up.

Logan wheeled around angrily. "You're not supposed to prank us back," he complained.

Zoey lifted her eyebrows, but before she could launch into it with Logan, a golf cart pulled up and Dean Rivers got out, followed by a very angry-looking man in a charcoal-gray suit. With them were Dean Rivers's secretary and a photographer.

"Uh-oh," Dana said softly. Dean Rivers looked shocked. His secretary looked appalled. The photographer simply looked through his lens at the well-dressed statue and started clicking away.

"Rivers!" the man in the suit was suddenly as red as his necktie. "Would you care to tell me why the statue of my father is wearing — that?!" he stammered, clearly horrified.

"Uh . . ." The dean looked around, hoping to find an answer on the students' faces.

Zoey and the girls tried to act casual, but inside Zoey was wigging out. This was *not* good. Operation Prank-Back had backfired . . . big-time!

"Oh, Daddy," Mr. Bradford cried, stepping closer to his father's gilded form, "what have they done to you!?"

The photographer circled the statue, still snapping away in an effort to capture every angle. Panicked, Dean Rivers snatched the camera from him.

"Don't take pictures!" he snarled. This was not a moment he wanted to remember.

"Here, let me get this off of you," Mr. Bradford said to his "father" as he reached up to pull the dress away. But what was underneath was even worse — matching underwear!

"Undergarments!" Mr. Bradford screamed in horror. He looked like a volcano about to erupt. And judging from the expression on his face, Dean Rivers was about to blow his top, too.

"Who did this?" Dean Rivers growled, looking right at Chase, Logan, and Michael. "I demand to know this instant!" Not only was his photo op ruined, the founder's son was hopping mad.

Logan looked smug. "I'll tell you who did it —"

"Nooo"—Chase cut Logan off and shot him a look—"because we don't know who did it, right?" He glanced over at Zoey, who looked really cute today in her red T-shirt and matching sneakers. He was not about to get her in trouble.

"I'm not taking the heat for this," Logan said under his breath. Michael was silent. He could not take his eyes off the statue.

"I'm not going to ask you again," Dean Rivers said, and leaned in close. "Who did this?"

"Uh." Chase hated to point out the obvious, but . . . "Technically, sir, you did just ask us again," he said, raising a finger in the air for emphasis.

Dean Rivers's mouth was pursed up like he'd been sucking lemons. "Chase —"

"Sorry!" Chase apologized, cutting off the impending lecture. What was he thinking? Dean Rivers was already furious.

Zoey was watching the whole scene with a growing knot in her stomach. As much as she wanted to be off the hook, she could not let the guys take the fall. This prank had been the girls' idea and they needed to step up and take the blame. She took a deep breath. "We did it," she blurted.

Suddenly everyone was staring at Zoey and her

friends. She shifted uncomfortably and tucked a lock of hair behind an ear.

"Who is *we*?" Dean Rivers seethed.

"Us girls," Dana said, taking her share of the heat. She couldn't let Zoey go down by herself.

"Well, I should have known," Mr. Bradford turned his fury on the girls. His face was still as red as a tomato.

"C'mon," Chase said, trying to defend his friends. "It was only a prank."

Mr. Bradford didn't seem to hear him. "This is what I get for allowing girls into Pacific Coast Academy," he fumed.

"All right, now, wait a second —" Zoey held up her hand. The girls hadn't started the tradition of Prank Week. They were only trying to get back at the boys.

"My father always intended for this school to be for boys only," Mr. Bradford said. He glared at the girls in front of him as if they were ants on his blueberry pie. "And so did I. But I let my wife talk me into letting girls in — which was my big mistake."

"Sir —" Zoey tried to interrupt. She could not believe her ears. Letting girls in to PCA was no mistake!

"Girls," Mr. Bradford snarled, "enjoy your next few months here at Pacific Coast Academy. Because after this semester, this school goes back to boys only."

Worst Nightmare

Zoey felt like she was drowning as she listened to Mr. Bradford go on and on about how girls should obviously never have been allowed at PCA. Sitting with Nicole and Dana in Dean Rivers's office, she tried not to look out the window at the shimmering Pacific or the gorgeous campus she thought of as her home.

"I meant what I said!" Mr. Bradford bellowed as he paced behind the dean's desk. "After this semester, no more girls at PCA."

Dean Rivers's sighed in frustration. He was beginning to feel like he was one of the students. "Mr. Bradford," he coaxed, "this was just a harmless prank."

"Harmless prank?" he echoed angrily. "They disgraced the memory of my daddy!"

"Sir, if I could just please explain —" Zoey began.

She had to get Mr. Bradford to hear their side! But he wasn't hearing anything at all.

"This is exactly what happens when you put teenage boys and teenage girls together. You know what you get?"

Zoey stared at him blankly. She could think of lots of answers — fun, a slice of life in the real world, a great school experience — but she doubted any of those were what Mr. Bradford had in mind.

"High jinks," Mr. Bradford said, answering his own question. "And I don't like high jinks. I like my jinks low." He made a slow, low, even-keeled gesture with his arm.

Zoey shook her head and glanced at her friends. What was he talking about?

"Look, we're really sorry," Dana tried. She was feeling unusually vulnerable. Sure, she acted as if she was annoyed with half the students at PCA. But the truth was, she loved it here. And the girls were holding their own, too. They were practically ruling the school! Leaving would be a total bummer.

"Please don't make me go back to my old school!" Nicole begged, leaning toward Mr. Bradford and lacing her fingers together. Just the thought of it freaked her out. "The boys there are all dumb and gross!"

"We swear it will never happen again," Zoey added, in case he wasn't getting the point that they would do almost anything to stay at PCA!

"Oh, I know," Mr. Bradford said with a stiff nod. "Because after this semester, you're gone. Pacific Coast Academy will once again be an institution for boys, and boys only."

"You can't do that!" Zoey protested, feeling completely desperate.

"Oh, yes, I can," Mr. Bradford replied smugly. "My father founded this school. I can put ducks in the toilets if I want to. Now, good day, girls." He strode to the door and left the office, closing the door behind him.

Zoey could barely breathe. Her worst nightmare was coming true. The girls were getting kicked out of PCA!

Getting to their feet, the girls filed out of Dean Rivers's office. They made their way across campus in silence.

Finally Zoey spoke. "I can't believe we got kicked out over a dumb statue," she said, still in shock.

"It's so not fair," Dana agreed miserably.

"Yeah," Nicole added. She dumped her pink backpack onto an outdoor bench and sat down dejectedly.

"Birds do way worse things to that statue every day and I don't see them getting kicked out." Her dark eyes welled with tears.

Zoey looked at Dana, not exactly sure what to do. She wanted to comfort Nicole but felt so terrible herself she wasn't sure she had it in her.

"Nicole," Zoey began, putting a consoling arm on her friend's back.

"I don't wanna leave!" Nicole cried, sobbing into the canvas of her backpack. "This is the best school ever. It's got a swimming pool and cute boys and it's across the street from the beach . . . and it has cute boys."

Zoey crouched down in front of the bench. "I'm sure there are cute boys back at your school in Kansas," she offered. It wasn't much, but it was all she could come up with.

Nicole looked at her friend through her tears. "No," Nicole insisted seriously. "They're all dumb and gross." Her lower lip trembled. "I wanna stay here at PCA!" she wailed.

Dana crossed her arms over her chest. Seeing Nicole so upset was really bumming her out. Who'd have guessed that she'd come to care so much about the perky girl who had woken her up every morning with her hair dryer the first week of school? "This is all the guys' fault!" she stated flatly.

"I know!" Zoey agreed. If it weren't for Prank Week, this whole mess never would have started. "Them and their stupid Prank Week," she fumed.

Just then, Quinn walked by, completely engrossed in her sonic Quinnvention.

"Quinn, did you hear?" Dana inquired.

"This is gonna be our last semester at PCA," Zoey finished. She still couldn't believe it was true.

Quinn barely looked up from her device. "Can't talk," she said with a devilish grin. Then, without even pausing, she walked away. "Plotting revenge" were the only words she mumbled.

Nicole sniffled and wiped her eyes. "I'm gonna miss her weird ways," she said forlornly.

Zoey squared her shoulders. "Okay, that's it," she said firmly. She knew what she had to do. "I'm gonna fix this right now." She got to her feet and strode away, leaving her friends looking after her in confusion.

Zoey sat squarely in her chair in Dean Rivers's office. The dean and Mr. Bradford were listening intently.

It was time to wrap up her confession speech with a good punch line.

"So, with all due respect, sir, I think it's wrong to blame all the girls at PCA when the whole thing was my idea." Zoey gulped. Leaving her friends behind would be torture, but a lot better than knowing she had gotten them all kicked out. After all, she was the one who had declared war on the boys.

"She does have a point, sir," Dean Rivers said.

"And so do I," Mr. Bradford boomed, still clearly angry. "My father's image was besmirched in front of the entire school!"

"But it was my idea!" Zoey said again. "I'm the besmudger . . . uh, smircher." She took a deep breath. Taking the rap for the statue prank might be the hardest thing she'd ever done. She hoped it would be worth it. "I think you should let the rest of the girls stay at PCA and kick me out. Just me."

Mr. Bradford was silent as he gave Zoey a hard stare. He looked at Dean Rivers seated behind his large wooden desk. "All right," he finally said. "Zoey Brooks, you're expelled."

"Mr. Bradford," Dean Rivers began.

"And the rest of the girls can stay?" Zoey asked.

Mr. Bradford thought for a minute. It was one of the longest minutes in Zoey's life. She hoped the last torturous half hour would be worth it. It just had to be.

"On one condition," Mr. Bradford said, driving a hard bargain.

"What?" Zoey asked, almost afraid to hear the answer. Mr. Bradford wasn't exactly a softie.

"You apologize," Mr. Bradford stated. He slipped his hands into his pockets and nodded slightly.

That didn't seem too terrible. "I'm sorry," Zoey offered, as sincerely as possible.

"No," Mr. Bradford said. "Not just to me. In front of the entire school. And then you leave."

Zoey gulped. She'd do it, of course, especially since she had no choice. She'd do anything to let her friends stay at PCA.

But she wasn't looking forward to it.

CHAPTER 7

Good-bye, PCA

Zoey picked up her purple PCA sweatshirt and shoved it into her suitcase. She still couldn't believe this was really happening. And judging from the fact that Nicole kept taking things back out of her suitcase, neither could her roommates.

"You're not leaving," Nicole said, pulling the sweatshirt off the packed pile.

"Yes, I am." Zoey reached for the sweatshirt. She was glad her roomies wanted her to stay, but they weren't helping. Leaving was going to be hard enough as it was.

Zoey put the sweatshirt back into her suitcase and added another pile of clothes on top. Nicole grabbed the whole pile and pulled it out.

"Nicole, will you stop unpacking me?" she said.

"No," Nicole said flatly. Zoey couldn't leave! She

was the best friend and roommate Nicole had ever had. Period.

"Yes," Zoey stated. She took the pile of clothes and set them back in her suitcase. At this rate, packing was going to take forever.

Dana pulled a shirt from the pile.

Not Dana, too! Zoey thought. She needed at least one of her roommates to be strong.

"Dana, you're gonna have to let me leave," Zoey said, feeling sad and exasperated at the same time. This whole situation was a total and complete bummer.

"I know," Dana replied. She gestured to the pink shirt she'd just pulled from Zoey's suitcase. "This is mine."

"Oh. Sorry," Zoey said.

Dana eyed the shirt for a second. "Here, you take it," she offered.

"You sure?" Zoey asked. It was a plain, hot-pink T-shirt with a great neckline. Zoey really liked it.

Dana handed it over. "Take it," she repeated.

"Thanks," Zoey said gratefully. She knew Dana liked the shirt, too. It was not like her to be so generous. Or mushy.

"This is so wrong!" Nicole burst out. "Zoey, you can't leave! It's —"

"Uh-oh, here come the waterworks," Dana quipped, trying to make light of the situation. The truth was, she wasn't that far from tears herself.

"I can't help it if I cry!" Nicole wailed. She stopped and felt her cheeks. They were dry. "Wait, no tears are coming out." She slapped herself in the back of the head, then felt her eyes. "Nothing!" she exclaimed. "I've cried myself dry!" Her face twisted into a tortured expression. "That's so sad!" she whimpered.

Suddenly there was a knock on the door, and Vicki came into the room. Her shiny dark hair was down and was so long it touched the bottom of her shirt.

"Hey, Zoey," she said dejectedly. "Ummm, there's a phone call for you in the lounge."

Zoey looked confused. People always called her in her room or on her cell. "Who calls me in the lounge?" she asked, giving her roommates the eye. What were they up to?

"C'mon," Dana coaxed. "Let's go down there."

Zoey shrugged and headed out the door with Dana on her heels. But Nicole was still worrying about her tear supply. She slapped the back of her head and felt her eyes again. Nothing. "How can I be out of tears?" she asked in disbelief. It seemed impossible, didn't it? She looked around, suddenly realizing that she was talking to no one. Her roommates had left the room! "Wait up!" she called, hurrying after them.

Zoey walked into the lounge and saw all the girls gathered together in front of a giant cake, complete with candles.

"What's goin' on?" she asked.

"We wanted to say thanks," one of her dorm-mates said.

"For fixing it so we can all stay here at PCA," Vicki explained.

Zoey blinked back tears. That was so sweet! She was really going to miss the PCA girls. She stepped forward to blow out the candles and noticed the writing on the cake.

"We'll miss you, Zowie?" she said, a little confused.

Vicki grinned sheepishly. "They misspelled it," she admitted. "Sorry."

Zoey smiled. She wished it were Zowie and not she who was leaving PCA. "It's okay." It was the thought that counted, right? She leaned forward and blew out the candles, then went over to her friends. "Thanks, guys," she said, giving them a group hug.

Nicole watched the girls embrace and waited for the tears to come. She waited, and waited . . .

"What's up?" a voice called as a group of guys came into the lounge, led by Michael, Chase, and Logan.

"Just sorta sayin' good-bye," Zoey replied with a sad shrug.

Chase stepped forward. There were so many things he wanted to tell her! "Listen, Zoey, we feel kinda bad, 'cause, I mean, the whole Prank Week thing kinda got outta hand, and, y'know, we didn't know anyone would — listen, uh, we didn't want you to, uh, you know what I'm sayin'?"

Michael gave Chase a look. "*You* don't even know what you're sayin'," he scoffed. Chase could babble like nobody's business, but when there was an actual message, he just couldn't get it out!

Michael took matters into his own hands and turned to the girls. "Look, Zoey, we just came by to say we think it stinks that you have to leave. And, uh, we got you something." He handed Zoey a big lime-green gift bag with tissue sticking out of the top.

Zoey reached inside and pulled out a stuffed bunny with a PCA shirt. She grinned. "Aw, it's a bunny with a PCA shirt on it."

"Chase picked it out," Logan said with a smirk.

"Okay, why tell people!?" Chase said, blushing with embarrassment.

"C'mon, let's eat the *Zowie* cake," Vicki suggested.

Nothing like a little cake to take your mind off of stuff. Everybody gathered around and got ready to dig in. Everybody but Chase and Michael.

"Well, go on, man." Michael looked at Chase expectantly and then motioned toward Zoey with his eyes.

"What?" Chase asked, his mouth barely moving.

Zoey glanced over and shot Chase a small smile.

"You know what." Michael gave Chase his patented "no duh" face. It was time for the guy to stop playing dumb. "C'mon. Zoey's leaving tomorrow. And if you don't tell her how you feel now, that's it. Last chance."

Chase looked at the floor. He looked up at Zoey, then back at the floor. She was a great friend. She was supercute. And she was leaving. Now would be the perfect time to tell her how much he cared, but —"Yeah, I dunno —" Chase started to tell Michael he wasn't sure, when a huge shove sent him flying in Zoey's direction. Now or never. "Hey," Chase said, catching his balance. So much for smooth entrances.

"Hey." Zoey held her bunny under her arm. Chase motioned her over to a quieter spot in the room. He looked a little nervous.

"Um, listen, Zoey." Chase shrugged. "I just wanted to say that I think it's been really cool getting to know you and . . . and hangin' with you and stuff . . . and playing foosball . . ." Before Chase met Zoey, he didn't even know girls liked foosball. She had been such a good friend. The more Chase talked, the more he realized how much he was going to miss her. "And, seein' movies and doin' homework together . . ." He knew he was rambling, but if he stopped talking now, he wouldn't be able to get to the part he really needed to say. "I kinda wanted to say something . . . would this be a good time?"

Zoey looked over Chase's shoulder, confused. The crowd was grubbing on cake. She and Chase were basically alone. "Well, yeah." Zoey shrugged. Why wouldn't it be a good time? "I'm standing right here."

"Yeah." Chase managed a small laugh and pointed at Zoey. "There you are, right there." But for how much longer?

"Hi." Zoey said. She was still waiting for him to get to the point.

"Hi." Chase waved. This was not exactly going well. "So what I wanted to say was —"

At that moment, Quinn ran into the room, holding her sonic neural neutralizing device in two hands. "I've done it! I've done it! I've done it!" she yelled.

Well, Chase thought, Quinn had certainly done something. She had interrupted him. Chase hoped it was worth it. He turned and watched Quinn, who was trying hard to contain her excitement, jump from one foot to the other in her cropped blue pants and funky shirt.

"None of you thought I could build a sonic neural neutralizer that would render people unconscious with sound waves, but I've done it. Now, when I activate this orb, you will all be knocked out, so try to fall on something soft," she cautioned them.

Chase scanned the room to see if anyone looked alarmed. They didn't.

"Ready?" Quinn pressed the button. Zoey started to protest. Then all around Chase, students pressed their hands to the sides of their heads, desperate to block out the earsplitting noise. The room — no, the whole building — was suddenly plunged into darkness.

"Is anybody unconscious?" Quinn's voice echoed out of the gloom.

"Noooo!" Dozens of annoyed voices answered her.

At least we can still hear, Chase thought as Quinn turned to storm out. He wondered if it was too late to tell

Zoey he liked her. He had a little time — if he could just figure out where she was. He thought he heard her breathing. Then he heard something else.

CRASH!

"Okay." Quinn hadn't made it out of the room yet. "Who put that lamp there?" she asked accusingly.

This was impossible. What Chase had to say was going to have to wait.

CHAPTER 8

All for One

Zoey stood miserably between Mr. Bradford the statue and Mr. Bradford the cranky guy in the suit. Her bags were packed. Her backpack was slung on her shoulders. She was almost ready to leave PCA — there was just one more thing to do.

In front of her, Dean Rivers was at a podium speaking into a microphone. "All right, students." Dean Rivers hushed the crowd. "Zoey would like to say a few words before she leaves PCA. Zoey?"

Taking a deep breath, Zoey approached the mic. This was not the way she had anticipated addressing her class. She'd been hoping to give a graduation speech one day, not an apology today.

"Fellow classmates," she began, "I just want to apologize to all of you and, most importantly, to Mr. Bradford and his family for dressing his father's statue up in ladies' clothes." Zoey had to look down at the podium for a second. Looking out into the eyes of her friends was killing her. "And I know it was very wrong and disrespectful, and I'm really, really sorry." Zoey finished her speech and walked out onto the lawn to stand with the other students, her *former* classmates. She felt sorrier than she had in her whole life to have to leave this place. But at least she knew the other girls would get to stay.

Nicole gave Zoey a hug as Mr. Bradford took the mic.

"Thank you, Miss Brooks." Mr. Bradford scowled. His close-cropped white hair gleamed in the southern California sun. "Now I'd like to say a few words about my father. Although he wasn't a good-looking man, my father had a great vision when he founded this school, Pacific Coast Academy."

In the sea of students, Logan, Chase, and Michael huddled together, barely listening to the speech.

"This is it," Michael whispered so only his friends could hear him.

"Here we go," Chase said softly. His heart was pumping. Logan pulled a small remote control out of his pack and pointed it toward the two Mr. Bradfords.

"Do it," Chase gave the order.

Logan hit the button. The remote beeped. And a stream of water shot from between the legs of Mr. Bradford-the-statue, making it look as if he were peeing on the manicured PCA lawn.

Suddenly Mr. Bradford-the-grump's speech was drowned out by the sound of laughter. He trailed off and turned around to see the latest addition to his father's statue. "What in the world?" he sputtered.

While the kids laughed, Mr. Bradford walked toward the gold man, trying to stop the flow of water. He looked like a kid in a sprinkler. Only angry. And wearing a wool suit instead of a swimsuit.

Zoey could not believe what she was seeing. What were those guys up to?

"Who did this? I demand to know who is responsible! Who did this?" Dripping wet and hopping mad, Mr. Bradford glared at the students. Nobody said a word.

Finally, Logan raised his hand. "I did."

Logan? Zoey couldn't believe it. Well, she could believe Logan would do something like this, but why?

"You!" Mr. Bradford fumed. "Well, let me tell you something, Mr.—"

"Wait!" Chase raised his hand next. "I helped him."

"Me, too." Michael stepped closer to his friends.

"Yeah." Chase was starting to smile. And Zoey was starting to catch on to their plan. "In fact, all of us guys did it together. C'mon," he shouted to the group, "raise your hand if you had anything to do with this!"

Behind Chase, every guy in the school added his hand to the sea of palms waving at Mr. Bradford.

Dana did not want to miss this one. And she didn't want the guys to get all of the credit, either. "It wasn't just the guys," she said loudly.

"Yeah, it was us, too!" Nicole raised her hand.

"Yeah, all of us." Vicki turned around to make sure the girls were onboard. They were. More hands were raised in the quad than she had ever seen up in an algebra class. In fact, every kid there had his or her hand in the air.

"Rivers!" Mr. Bradford yelled for the dean.

"Well, what do you want me to do, sir?" Dean Rivers held up his hand like a criminal surrendering. "Expel them all?"

"He's right," Chase said. "If you expel Zoey, you have to expel all of us."

The kids all stood together nodding in agreement. It was a standoff.

For a minute, Zoey thought Mr. Bradford's head

might explode just like the water balloon that had started this war. Then he actually managed to say something reasonable.

"All right! Just stop my daddy from peeing," Mr. Bradford said, sounding a little choked up, "and no one gets expelled."

With the touch of a button on Logan's remote, the stream of water stopped flowing. Everyone cheered loudly. There were high fives and hugs. It was an awesome moment for everyone but Mr. Bradford.

"Rivers! I think I'm having a spell. Drive me to the clinic," he said, sounding woozy.

"Yes, sir." While Mr. Bradford and the dean made a hasty exit, Zoey found her way over to Chase and gave him a huge hug.

"Chase! You're the best!" She beamed.

"Uh, thanks." Chase shrugged. He was grateful for the hug, and wished he could take the credit. "But actually, it wasn't my idea."

"Michael?" If it wasn't Chase's idea, Zoey knew it had to be Michael's.

"Not me." Michael raised his eyebrows.

"Then who?" Zoey was confused. What other guy would come up with such a great, and risky, plan to keep her in school?

Michael swung his arms around in a circle, stopping with both of his index fingers pointing at Logan.

Wait, was this another prank? "Logan?" Zoey asked in disbelief.

Logan shrugged modestly and waited for the thanks and hugs he was sure would be coming his way any second. He deserved every last one, of course.

"Why would you help me stay at PCA?" Zoey asked. Hadn't he been the guy trying to get girls, and especially her, out of here since day one?

"Ah, if you weren't here, who else would I pick on?" Logan quipped out of the corner of his mouth.

Zoey grinned back. He had a point. Picking on her was his favorite pastime.

Things were about to get back to normal when Quinn came running up to the group of students. She had her sonic machine in her hand.

"I've done it! I've done it! I've done it! I've perfected the sonic neural neutralizer! It's time for revenge on the boys." Quinn held her invention close to her chest just like a mad scientist in a movie.

Dana, Nicole, and Vicki rolled their eyes in unison.

"Quinn, will ya stop?" Nicole asked.

"It's over," Dana said bluntly. The girl needed to let this neural neutralizer thing *go*.

Quinn looked baffled.

Zoey tried to explain what Quinn had missed while she was busy in her lab. "Yeah, the guys helped us. I can stay at PCA!"

"We don't need your neural neutralizer thingy," Nicole said.

"Which wouldn't have worked, anyway," Dana added with a shrug.

"Fine. Make me do all this work for nothing." Quinn pitched her invention into the trash and stormed off.

"That girl's just a little bit nuts," Chase said, watching her go.

"Yeah, she is," Zoey had to agree. It was weird. Quinn was so smart, it was scary, but how come her inventions never seemed to work?

Suddenly an indescribable noise echoed out of the trash can. Before anyone could cover their ears, every kid in the area fell to the lawn — unconscious.

This time Quinn *had* done it.

Special Delivery

It took only a few minutes for the effect of the neutralizer to wear off enough for the students to regain consciousness. But even days later Zoey swore that she still felt kind of fuzzy-headed. What she needed after all the stress of almost being expelled, the prank war, and getting knocked out was some serious relaxation time. Game night with the girls was just what the doctor ordered!

"Okay, Zoey, you're up." Dana handed Zoey a pair of dice so she could take her turn. She, Nicole, Vicki, and Dana had just started a round of Confess or Stress.

Zoey shook the dice, hoping for "confess." She'd had enough stress to last a lifetime. "Here we go." She rolled. The dice tumbled across the table and came up double threes.

"Six. Even," Nicole said with a grin. She loved

playing Confess or Stress and was always excited to find out what was going to happen next.

"Confess!" Vicki said. She hoped Zoey was going to spill something good.

Zoey racked her brain for a seriously embarrassing moment she could share. Oh, yeah, she had one. "Okay, one time when I was ten"— Zoey could feel her cheeks getting warmer just talking about it —"I burped in church."

The girls cracked up.

"Eww."

"Gross."

"If that happened to me, I'd die," Nicole said, taking a sip of water. She hated to do anything embarrassing, ever.

Quinn, on the other hand . . .

"Hey, Quinn." Nicole spotted their resident science nerd crossing the lounge and invited her over. "You wanna play Confess or Stress with us?"

"How do you play?" Quinn asked, looking from one girl to another. She was always curious about new things.

"You roll the dice," Zoey explained, twirling the key she always wore around her neck.

"And if you get an even number, you have to confess something really embarrassing," Dana went on.

"And if you roll an odd number, you have to do something stressful," Nicole finished.

"Like eat a poisonous bug?" Quinn asked. She was liking the sound of this game.

"Stressful. Not lethal," Zoey said to clarify, shooting Nicole and Dana a look. Quinn always managed to take things to the next strange level.

"Oh, and the most important rule: Nothing that anyone says leaves this room." Nicole looked into Quinn's big brown eyes. That part was serious.

"Gotta swear," Zoey said.

Raising her hand like a good Girl Scout, Quinn swore, and then plunked down on the couch next to Zoey.

"My turn!" Nicole reached for the dice.

"Wait," Quinn said. "I'm starved. Can we order some sushi?"

"Already on the way," Zoey said slowly, leaning back into the soft cushions. The night was shaping up just right.

"How cool is it that we have our own sushi bar right on campus?" Nicole asked. Life at PCA could not get any better.

"The coolest," Zoey confirmed. Sushi Rox rocked!

"Except that their delivery guy is Logan," Dana

scowled, balancing on the arm of the couch in her signature dark colors — gray tank over a black tee.

"Logan?" Even Quinn looked disgusted at the mention of his name, and she was hard to gross out. "He's such a jerk."

"And speak of the jerk." Dana motioned toward the door with her eyes. Logan was just coming in, dressed in his blue Sushi Rox delivery uniform and looking full of himself, as usual.

"'Sup, ladies?" he asked, walking slowly over to the game with his arms open wide so everyone could admire his uniform. He looked good in everything, of course.

"We were just talking about you," Zoey said honestly, shooting a smirk at the girls.

"Yeah." Logan shrugged. "I can't blame ya." He just assumed the world stood in awe of his greatness . . . if he only knew what they'd really been saying.

"Where's our sushi?" Dana demanded, looking at Logan's empty hands. If Logan did not have her California roll, there was no reason for him to be here.

"Oh, one sec." Logan turned back toward the door and snapped his fingers impatiently. A second guy with an enormous box struggled in. "C'mon, let's go, let's go, let's go."

The poor guy with the box barely made it into the room. When he looked out from behind the huge box of sushi, Zoey was surprised to see Chase's face. She had no idea he'd taken a job at Sushi Rox.

"You know, you could help me," Chase pointed out to Logan, still balancing the box by himself.

"Yeeeah." Logan pretended to consider it for about a second. "No, thanks." Why would he do any of the work if he could get out of it?

"You're working with Logan now?" Zoey asked. She kind of wondered why Chase hung out with Logan so much.

"Well." Chase shot Logan a look. "*I'm* working. He seems to be watching."

"I'm training you so you can learn to make deliveries on your own." Logan said it like he was doing Chase a huge favor.

"Good." Zoey flashed Logan a game-show host smile. "Now that we know you're not delivering anymore, we'll order more often."

Dana and the other girls cracked up. But Logan was not deterred. "All right, all right." He held up his hands in mock defeat. "Look, I know there's been a little tension between me and you girls since you came to PCA."

"Ya think?" Zoey asked sarcastically. Logan had a long, dark history with her and the other girls. He was always stirring up trouble — like trying to keep them off the basketball team. Most of the time, it seemed like he didn't even *want* girls at PCA.

"Yes," Logan said earnestly. "And I feel bad about that — which is why I wanna give you something." Logan stepped out into the hall.

Zoey looked at her friends. Was he kidding? She could not figure him out. First he didn't want girls at PCA, then he kept her from getting expelled, and now he wanted to give them a gift? Was this for real? When Logan came back in, he was carrying a giant teddy bear wearing a PCA T-shirt.

"Just a present from me to you girls for your lounge here," Logan said modestly.

Dana still was not buying it. "You're giving *us* a present?" she asked suspiciously.

"Yeah. That so weird?" Logan asked.

"Kinda." Zoey nodded. "Chase, was this your idea?" That would definitely make more sense.

"Nope, I had nothing to do with it. It was all him." Chase looked as baffled as Zoey felt.

"Wow. This is really nice of you, Logan." Maybe the

school's biggest jerk was actually turning over a new leaf. Anything's possible, right?

"Hey," Logan said with a shrug, "I figure we're all at the same boarding school, we might as well be nice to one another."

Wow. Zoey looked at Nicole. Logan was full of surprises. She didn't know he could be so . . . human.

"Perfect." Logan put the big bear in a seat of honor looking out over the whole lounge. He gave the bear's head a little tweak so its cute fuzzy face was looking right at Zoey and her friends.

"Well, we gotta jam," Chase said from behind his box. It was getting really heavy.

"Um, Chase?" Zoey called before the guys got out the door. "Can we have our sushi?"

"Oh, right! I'm always forgetting that part." Chase handed Nicole the covered plastic platter from the top of his box — the whole reason they'd come to the girls' dorm. "Your sushi," he offered.

"Your money." Since his hands were full, Nicole put the bills in Chase's mouth. It only took Logan half a second to snatch them out and pocket them.

Zoey waved good-bye. But before the guys got out the door, Logan stopped Chase again.

"Oh, hey, man," Logan spoke softly and shook his head apologetically at Chase. "I'm feelin' kinda sick, so I'm gonna head back to the dorm and lie down."

"What?" Chase could hardly believe his ears, or his aching arms. "I can't deliver all of this sushi by myself." It was his first night!

"You'll be fine." Logan punched Chase on the shoulder and sauntered out of the lounge, looking amazingly healthy.

"Great, all alone with forty pounds of raw fish." Chase peered into the big box of sushi trays and spotted something glistening and slimy. "And whatever that orange stuff is," he added with a shiver.

CHAPTER
10

Confess or Stress

Once the guys left, the night really got on a roll. They had all the sushi they could eat, and it was Nicole's turn to throw the dice!

Zoey put down her chopsticks. The dice landed on six and two. "Eight," Zoey announced. "Nicole, confess!"

"Come on," Quinn said between bites of sushi. She could not wait to hear Nicole spill her guts. She wasn't sure why, but most of the girls didn't confide their secrets to her. "You gotta do it!" she squealed.

"Okay." Nicole sat up straighter and looked around knowingly. The girls near her leaned in a little to hear better. "You know how I have study hall with almost all guys, right?" Everyone nodded. This could be good. "Well, I kinda made a chart of which guys have the cutest lips." She giggled.

Zoey had to laugh. Nicole could be downright

goofy sometimes. Or maybe she just had too much time on her hands in study hall!

"You rated boys' lips?" Quinn could not believe it. But it might have some scientific merit. "On what criteria?" she asked.

Nicole shrugged. "Shape. Color. Cuteness."

Of course! What else would you rate lips on? Everyone laughed again.

"Okay, okay. It's Zoey's turn again," Nicole said when the giggling died down.

"Dice me." Zoey held out her hand and threw the dice.

"Odd," Dana called out. Stress time.

"Now, how should we stress Zoey?" Quinn asked, raising her eyebrows. The look in her eyes was making Zoey a little nervous. She'd seen that look, right before she had become the guinea pig for one of Quinn's Quinnventions.

"I say . . ." Nicole thought for second. "Zoey has to prank-call Mr. Callahan."

"Yeah, yeah." Dana nodded. That was a good one.

"That'd be so great!" Quinn approved.

"I'm not prank-calling our English teacher." Zoey shook her head. They had to be kidding.

"You rolled odds," Dana pointed out.

"You gotta face the stress." Quinn tapped her chopsticks on her plate. It was all part of the game.

"I don't have his phone number." Zoey tried once more to get out of it. But Nicole had come to tonight's round of Confess or Strees prepared. She held up a slip of paper and raised her eyebrows.

Zoey sighed. There was no wiggling out of this one. She took the paper and pulled the lounge phone over to their table. She hit the speaker button and dialed.

"Hello?" Mr. Callahan answered.

"Yes," Zoey said in her best southern accent. "I'm callin' about the mustard you ordered?"

Dana held her hand over her mouth to keep from laughing. Zoey's accent was hilarious.

"Mustard?" Mr. Callahan was confused. "I didn't order any mustard."

"Uh, yes, sir, you ordered nine thousand jars of mustard," Zoey drawled sweetly.

"What? Who could eat that much mustard?" Mr. Callahan was starting to lose his cool. The girls, meanwhile, were struggling not to crack up.

"That's none of my business." Now Zoey was smiling herself. This was kind of fun. "So what time would you like me to drop off the mustard?"

"I don't even *like* mustard!" Mr. Callahan yelled.

"So why'd you order so much?" Zoey asked.

Luckily Mr. Callahan was so mad about the massive amount of mustard coming to his house, he did not hear Zoey and her friends collapse into fits of giggles.

Nicole, Zoey, and Chase sat outside at a round table, doing homework. The sun was shining. Overhead, seagulls swooped and screeched. The smell of the ocean was in the air. It was another gorgeous day at PCA.

Looking through her big brown shades, Zoey put down her book. She needed a little break from her studies. "So how was work last night?" she asked, turning toward Chase.

"Brutal," Chase answered. "Broo-tal." He broke it down phonetically to make his point.

"Delivering sushi is brutal?" Zoey asked. *This* she had to hear.

"It is when Logan goes home sick and I have to make thirty-two deliveries by myself," Chase explained.

"Whoa." Nicole did not like the sound of that. It sounded like hard work, something she tried to avoid.

"Yeah. Do you know how big this campus is?" Chase asked. *He* sure did. "I bet I had to walk ten miles." He held up all ten fingers to illustrate.

"What's going on, guys?" Logan was suddenly standing at their table with Michael and Brad.

"Just doin' some homework." Nicole smiled at the guys. They smiled back, obviously stifling laughter.

Zoey eyed the boys. Logan didn't look as if he'd been sick. In fact, he looked pretty darn happy and healthy. Too happy. He couldn't stop laughing and elbowing his friends.

"What's so funny?" Zoey finally asked.

"Oh, nothin', nothin'." Brad shrugged. But Zoey saw him try to catch Logan's eye. It was definitely *somethin'*.

"Yeah, we were jut wondering which one of us you think has the cutest lips," Michael said. All three of the boys puckered up and posed for the table.

Zoey tried to act as if the comment was totally normal. But she could see Nicole's look of pure panic through her friend's pink-tinted sunglasses.

"Um, why do you ask that?" Nicole asked nervously. This couldn't be a coincidence. Somebody had blabbed her confess!

"Just wondering," Logan said, acting aloof again as he waved the question off. "Just wondering . . ."

"Yeah, we gotta go." Michael led the guys away from the table. They left, slapping one another and laughing loudly.

Suddenly Logan turned back. "Oh, Zoey," he said as if he'd just remembered something, "I need to call Mr. Callahan at home. Would you happen to have his phone number?" Logan had mischief in his eyes. He looked at Zoey, who was openmouthed, and then turned and walked away without waiting for an answer.

That sealed it. Logan and his cronies knew a little too much about what the girls had been up to the night before.

Chase watched the whole exchange. He was baffled. "Okay, what was that all about?" He felt as if he had walked into a foreign film with no subtitles. Nobody was making sense. And Nicole and Zoey looked mad.

"I don't know." Nicole slammed down her pencil with a sigh.

"But we're going to find out." Zoey scowled, folding her arms across her chest.

CHAPTER 11

Tell All

"Did you tell?" Zoey marched into the girls' dorm lounge. She walked straight up to Dana, who was sitting on the couch, fixing her skateboard.

"Did you?" Nicole echoed. She was right behind Zoey and just as mad.

Dana scowled at her friends. She had no idea what they were talking about. "Tell who what?" she asked.

"The guys. About her cute-lip chart?" Zoey was talking so fast her blond braids were bobbing.

"Shhhh!" Nicole took her hands off her hips and held them palms down. Then she took a quick look around to make sure nobody else heard about the chart.

"And about me prank-calling Mr. Callahan?" Zoey went on in a whisper.

"No." Dana stopped working on her skateboard

long enough to glare at her roommates. Why were they accusing her?

"Well, *someone* told," Nicole said as she crossed her arms over the pink shirt that matched her pink skirt and glasses. She loved things that were coordinated.

"'Cause Michael and Logan know," Zoey explained to Dana.

"Well, I kept my mouth shut." Dana rolled her eyes. She was not a bigmouth, and Nicole and Zoey should know that. Uh, hello!

"Okay. Who blabbed?" Quinn stomped up to the three girls, holding a small green jar and looking upset.

"Blabbed what?" Zoey asked.

"You know — that I still like to eat baby food!" Quinn said, sounding as close to embarrassed as Zoey had ever heard her. The night before, she'd confessed that pureed foods were a major source of comfort during stressful times.

"It wasn't us." Zoey shook her head. She wondered how many other secrets had gotten out.

"Well," Quinn went on as she pried the lid off her small jar of baby food, "people know about it, and it is really upsetting!" She lifted her spoon and scooped a mushy green bite out of the jar. She paused. Nicole, Zoey, and Dana were all watching with looks of mild disgust.

"Pureed peas?" she offered, jabbing a red plastic spoon toward Nicole's face. She really wanted the whole jar to herself, but it was good to share with your friends.

Nicole and Zoey stared at the spoon. Nicole gulped and leaned away from the slimy green stuff. Both girls shook their heads.

Quinn shrugged. Excellent. There was more for her then, she thought as she shoveled a bite in her mouth and tried to forget her humiliation.

Chase walked into Sushi Rox, pulling on his delivery hat. His shell necklace was just visible under the polo-collared Rox shirt.

Behind the sushi bar the chef was dressed in purple with a matching headband tied around his forehead. He was slicing furiously.

"What's up, Kazu?" Chase greeted.

"You're late," Kazu replied with a loud whack of his huge knife.

Late? Chase checked his watch. "I'm ten minutes early," he said.

"No back sass!" Kazu shouted, holding the knife so it pointed straight up into the air.

"Okay." Chase smiled uneasily and held up a hand. "Just put the knife down," he requested.

Kazu pointed to a huge pile of trays sitting on the counter. "Now hurry, you have many deliveries to make."

Chase took a big stack. "No problem. I'll just take half of them. When Logan gets here, he can —"

"Logan's not coming." Kazu shook his head as he prepared more sushi.

"What?" Chase asked.

"He called in sick," Kazu explained.

"Again?" There was no way Logan was sick again, unless he was just sick of working. "Great. I have to make all of these deliveries by myself?" Chase asked.

"*Hie!*" Kazu nodded sharply. Chase bit his lip and took that for a yes.

"Okay, who's this huge order for?" Chase looked at the tag attached to the biggest tray in the bunch. It read DELIVER TO: LOGAN REESE. "Logan," Chase sighed. Of course.

"Okay, this is the funniest show ever." Zoey sat between Quinn and Nicole on the couch in the lounge, holding her stomach.

"The best." Nicole nodded in agreement before dipping her chip in the big bowl of guacamole on the table.

Coming back from the laundry room, Vicki held up a pair of Hello Bunny underwear. "Nicole, you left these in the dryer," she said.

"Oh." Nicole looked at the underwear, and then at all of the girls in the lounge who had turned to see what she forgot in the dryer. "Those aren't mine," she said quickly, her cheeks reddening.

Vicki smiled knowingly. "I'm pretty sure you're the only girl here who wears Hello Bunny underwear," she said.

Zoey giggled. Nicole was definitely the only girl who sported Hello Bunny.

With a sniff, Nicole swiped the undies out of Vicki's hand. "They were on sale," she said defensively, stuffing them in her back pocket to keep them out of sight.

Zoey and Quinn looked at their laps to hide their smiles.

"It's not funny!" Nicole snapped.

"Right," Zoey said, taking a bite of a chip.

"Sorry," Quinn agreed with a giggle.

"And Dana shouldn't be leaving her skateboard here." Nicole grabbed the board off the table to try and shift the focus off Hello Bunny. "People put food on this table."

Zoey hoped Nicole wasn't going to tell her to move

her bare feet next. They had been propped up on the table since the start of the show. Luckily Nicole didn't seem to notice her feet. But Quinn did.

"Hey, Zoey, what's up with your toenail?" Quinn asked, squinting at Zoey's toes.

"Oh," Zoey answered, "when I was seven, I dropped a bowling ball on it."

"Hmmm. Looks like a corn chip," Quinn remarked.

Zoey glared. A corn chip? What a weird — and gross — thing to say!

"I like corn chips!" Quinn gulped, catching Zoey's harsh gaze.

A second later, Dana walked in. "Hey, have any of you seen my skateboard? I thought I left it here on the —" All of a sudden, Dana stopped talking and started falling. She'd been so busy checking the table, she forgot to watch where she was going and stepped right on the thing she was looking for. The skateboard shot out from under her foot. Dana pitched forward, catching herself on the table, but not before her whole face slammed into the huge bowl of guacamole. When she pulled her face out, she was covered in thick green goo. She looked like she was getting a spa facial — only *a lot* less relaxed.

"Okay," she said slowly between gritted teeth. "Who left my skateboard there?"

76

Nicole looked at Zoey, her eyes full of terror. She knew what Dana was like when she was mad and clean. But mad and covered in guac? It was not going to be pretty!

"If I were you, I'd run," Zoey quickly counseled her friend.

Nicole wasted no time. She took off for the stairs, with the creature from the green lagoon right behind her. "Don't touch me!" Nicole screamed. Zoey didn't think Dana would comply.

CHAPTER 12
Cat Fight

The next day at lunch, Dana's mood had improved, but only slightly. "What are they laughing about?" Dana glared over her shoulder at a group of guys who were laughing loudly and looking at the table where Zoey, Nicole, and Dana were sitting with their lunch trays.

"I dunno," Zoey said, eyeing Nicole's tray. "You gonna eat those grapes?" Zoey pointed to the bunch on Nicole's plate.

"I was. Why, you want 'em?" Nicole asked. Zoey was gaga for grapes.

"No," Zoey answered, but she kept looking at the grapes until Nicole picked them up and plopped them on her plate.

"Yay," Zoey chirped, popping a grape in her mouth.

"Hey, Nicole." Brad cruised by the table and

paused to say hi. He had a shaggy surfer cut and sleepy-looking eyes, and wore a sporty jersey tee.

"Oh, hi, Brad." Nicole waved. Then she turned to Zoey and whispered, "He's on my cute-lip chart." Zoey could see why. When the girls looked back up, Brad was still there. "What's up?" Nicole asked.

"Oh, I was just wonderin'." Brad held up a pair of blue boxer shorts. They had Hello Bunny cutouts sewn all over them. The stitches around the cutouts were pretty sloppy — definitely a home job. "Do you like Hello Bunny?" He snickered and walked away, not even waiting for Nicole to answer.

With her mouth hanging open in shock and embarrassment, Nicole couldn't have said anything if she wanted to. It was all too much.

"Hey, Dana, you're pretty coordinated." A second guy approached their table — Darrell. He had his skateboard in his hand. "Tell me, is this the right way to ride a skateboard?" Darrell put the board on the ground and pretended to step on it and lose his balance. "Whoa!" He flailed his arms and took a pratfall on their table.

Dana slammed down her burger and helped herself to two fistfuls of Darrell's red button-down shirt. She pulled him close so she was looking him right in the face even though he was bigger and taller than she was.

"Okay, I want to know who told you and I want to know now," she demanded.

"Whaddya mean?" Darrell played dumb. He was pretty brave for a guy in Dana's clutches. Zoey pushed back her chair and stood up. She had Dana's back.

"She asked you a question," Zoey said angrily.

"Hey, hey. Easy there, corn-chip toe!" Darrell laughed.

Now it was Zoey's turn to be mortified. The girls all looked at one another. Something was going on, for sure. The guys seemed to know *everything*! And the girls did not like it one bit. It had to stop.

"All right, that's it!" Zoey yelled. "All girls in the dorm lounge!" she ordered. "Now!"

Every girl in the PCA dorm crowded into the lounge. They were all talking at once. It was total chaos!

Zoey climbed onto the couch. "Girls! All right! Girls!" she yelled. Zoey could barely hear herself, and there was no way she was going to get everyone's attention like this. Putting two fingers in her mouth, Zoey whistled as loud as she could. The talking stopped. Everyone turned to stare at the blond girl in the pink number 7 tank and turquoise jeans. Zoey had their attention.

"How does she do that?" Quinn squinted up at Zoey in wonder. Quinn could do a lot of things — like render the whole school unconscious — but she had never been able to whistle.

"Now, look," Zoey said, gazing around at the mob of angry girls, "someone in the girls' dorm is spreading secrets all over the PCA campus."

"And we're gonna find out who." Dana had her arms crossed over her black cap-sleeve tee. She looked from girl to girl to girl suspiciously.

"How?" Vicki asked. There were so many girls in the dorm that finding the fink seemed like finding a needle in a haystack. Practically impossible.

"Hey, I invented my own lie detector machine," Quinn volunteered, "and it's over ninety-eight percent accurate."

That sounded good. "How's it work?" Nicole asked.

"Well, I just connect three wires from the machine to your brain, so I can —"

Zoey cut Quinn off. "Wait — how do you connect the wires to our brains?" she asked.

"Oh, I only have to make a small incision just below your left ear so that I can —"

Nicole cut Quinn off. It wasn't sounding so good anymore. "Incision?" Nicole gasped.

"Quinn, nobody's taking a lie detector test if you have to do surgery on their head!" Zoey pointed at her head with both hands. There was no way Quinn and a scalpel were coming anywhere near it.

"It's one incision!" Quinn said, like it was no big deal. What a bunch of babies!

Climbing up on the couch next to Zoey, Vicki turned to the girls. "Hey, if Zoey's so afraid to take a lie detector test, maybe that's 'cause she's the one who's been spreading our personal secrets!"

The crowd started nodding and pointing, like they'd found the culprit.

What? Zoey could not believe her ears. "I'm one of the victims!" she said loudly. "Why would I spread secrets about myself?"

"To trick us!" Nicole shouted.

"Nicole!" Zoey's roommate was ready to turn her in! So much for friendship!

"Well." Nicole shrugged. *Somebody* had been telling secrets and it wasn't her.

With all the finger pointing, yelled accusations, and hurt feelings, the dorm lounge began to look like the ring of a wrestling match gone crazy. Everyone was so busy shouting, nobody noticed the giant teddy bear in the corner and his glowing red eye as he silently captured every moment. . . .

"Oh, oh, yes, yes. This is awesome." In his dorm room, Logan was loving it. He had a live Web feed of everything that was going on, or should he say "wrong" in the girls' lounge. When he took the teddy bear over to them, they had no idea it wasn't really a peace offering. It was really spy equipment. And the fun hadn't stopped since!

"I dunno, man." Michael was sitting next to Logan, staring at his open laptop and the action over at the girls' dorm. "I'm startin' to feel a little guilty about this."

"C'mon, man, this is classic!" Logan could not believe Michael was going to let his conscience get in the way of fun. Especially this much fun. Who would want to miss this?

On-screen, Vicki and Zoey were still going at it. "Why didn't you take the lie detector test?" Vicki demanded, getting in Zoey's face.

"Because, I'm not letting Quinn operate on my head!" Zoey yelled.

"It's one incision!" Vicki argued.

"Hey, aren't you supposed to be at work helping

Chase deliver sushi?" Michael interrupted Logan's viewing.

"Nah, I called in sick again," Logan said. He didn't want to miss a minute of his favorite new show. "Oh, this could turn into a real fight." He leaned in closer to the screen.

"I know, Zoey's about to mix it up with that girl Vicki." Michael shoved Logan with his shoulder to get a better view. "Zoom in, zoom in!" he demanded.

"'Kay, hang on." Logan pulled the Webcam in tighter. Vicki and Zoey weren't the only girls about to mix it up. Dozens of screaming girls were gesturing wildly at one another. "This is great!" Logan grinned. "You gotta love having girls here at PCA."

"I know, man, right?" Michael's guilty conscience was forgotten as he took in the scene. Only one girl stood alone, shoveling baby food into her mouth. Obviously Quinn could not take the stress.

Who's the Spy?

Zoey paced back and forth in her room. Things were not looking good. All the girls were fighting. All the guys knew the girls' secrets. Everyone was totally stressed out. She turned to Nicole and Quinn. "Okay, here's what we know," she began. "Somebody in the girls' dorm is telling our secrets all over campus."

Nicole was lying on Zoey's bed. Her eyes were wide. This was serious. Half the school knew about her cute-lip list. "Right," she said gravely.

"Now, what else do we know?" Zoey inquired. The sooner they got to the bottom of this, the better.

Next to Nicole, Quinn spooned up a bite of baby food. "The peas taste way better than pureed squash," she said, making a grossed-out face.

Zoey rolled her eyes. "Quinn, put the baby food

down and focus," she said firmly. Sometimes it seemed like the girl was on another planet.

Quinn sheepishly put the jar down behind her, then quickly picked it up again and shoveled a few more spoonfuls into her mouth. The peas *were* better, but the pureed squash kind of grew on you.

Nicole leaned away from the jar of squash. She might wear Hello Bunny underwear, but she drew the line at baby food. And, anyway, they really needed to think. Their reputations were on the line! "Okay," she said thoughtfully. "Why would one of the other girls sell us out?"

"I dunno." Zoey shrugged. That was the thing that had been bugging her. The girls in the dorm got along pretty well and knew they were all in the same boat at PCA. There were a lot more guys than girls, and everyone was still getting used to living together on one campus.

Zoey was quiet, thinking. Then, "Wait, when did this start happening?" she asked, sitting down on the edge of the bed.

Nicole tilted her head to the side. "Um . . . oh, a few nights ago," she remembered. "When we were playing Confess or Stress."

Quinn nodded, her glasses slipping down her nose a tiny bit. "Yeah, the night we ordered sushi."

"And Logan brought us that big teddy bear," Nicole finished.

The girls were silent as those words — and their meaning — sank in. A second later, Zoey was on her feet. Something smelled foul, and it wasn't old sushi.

A few minutes later, Nicole, Zoey, and Quinn crept up to the teddy bear, being careful not to get in front of it. Quinn led the way, holding a high-tech scanning device complete with blinking lights. It looked a little like a walkie-talkie with a round spatula on the end.

Quinn turned back to the other girls. "Ready?" she whispered.

Zoey put a finger to her lips. They couldn't let the camera pick up their voices, either!

Quinn nodded and punched several numbers into the device. Then she stepped forward and scanned the bear. The scanner beeped and blinked, especially near the bear's head.

Quinn pulled the scanner back and examined the readout. "That jerk," she said under her breath.

Zoey was dying to know what Quinn had found. "What?" she whispered.

"What's it say?" Nicole peered at the beeping gadget.

Quinn pointed away from the bear. "Go!" she whispered. Nicole led the way out of the lounge, motioning for her friends to follow. They raced upstairs and into Zoey and Nicole's room, slamming the door behind them.

"Well?" Zoey asked impatiently.

"That bear is broadcasting both audio and visual transmissions via broadband wavelengths to a remote digital receiver," Quinn said huffily.

"I knew it!" Nicole said, pointing a finger for emphasis. Then she wrinkled her nose in confusion. "What does that mean?" she asked.

Zoey looked to Quinn. "In English," she instructed.

"There's a wireless Webcam in that bear," Quinn stated simply.

"I knew it!" Nicole said again. Then her face scrunched up a second time. "Wait, I still don't know what that means," she admitted sheepishly.

Zoey waved her arms in frustration. "It means somebody's spying on everything we say and do in the girls' lounge." And it wasn't hard to figure out who: a complete and total class-A jerk. Logan. There was only one other question: Did he commit this horrible crime alone or did he have an accomplice?

Zoey crossed the campus so fast her blond hair flew behind her. Three minutes later, she stood outside Chase's (and Michael's and Logan's) room. Not bothering to knock, she burst through the door.

Chase was so surprised by the intrusion, he almost fell off his bed.

"Did you have anything to do with it?" Zoey demanded, planting her hands on her hips and giving Chase a good glare.

"Uh, come on in?" Chase replied, wondering what she was talking about. He was always happy to see Zoey, but sometimes the girl could be a little intense. Not to mention intimidating.

"Did you put a camera in that bear!?" She practically yelled. What was with this innocent act? He was Logan's roommate, for goodness' sake!

Add loud to that last list, Chase thought. He still had no clue about what was going on, except that Zoey was totally peeved. And she wasn't fun when she was peeved. "I don't think so," Chase said honestly. "Seeing as I don't have a camera. Or a bear."

Zoey was not convinced. How could he not know? "Chase —" Zoey began.

Chase shook his dark curly head. He was innocent! Why didn't Zoey trust him? "Will you just tell me what's goin' on here?" he interrupted, getting a little irritated himself.

"That bear you and Logan gave us?" Zoey said, tapping her foot impatiently. She folded her arms across her chest. "It's got a Webcam in it."

"What?!" Chase cried. Logan was a schemer, but this was low — even for him.

"Don't act like you don't know," Zoey said hotly, giving Chase yet another hard look.

Chase threw up his hands. "I'm not acting!" he proclaimed. He looked at Zoey steadily. She should know him better than this! "Zoey," he began.

Zoey stared Chase in the eye. He really did look innocent. And he was her friend. Zoey checked out the rest of the dorm room. Chase might not be guilty, but Logan was another story. And she was about to prove it.

"Where's Logan's computer?" she asked.

Chase wasn't sure he was liking where this was going, but he knew Zoey well enough not to try and stand in her way.

"Uh, over there," he said, pointing.

Zoey stepped across the room and sat down at Logan's computer.

"What are you looking for?" Chase asked, peering over her shoulder at the screen.

It took only a few clicks to find the evidence she was searching for. Zoey stared at the screen in disgust. There, right in front of her face, was the girls' lounge, complete with several female PCA students hanging out. "This," she said flatly. "See? The girls' lounge."

Chase's eyes widened as he looked at the screen. Then they narrowed in annoyance. "So this is why Logan's been blowing off work every night," he said, slapping his hand on his knee. Suddenly it was all coming together. Zoey and the girls were not the only ones being duped.

"Huh?" Zoey asked, turning to Chase.

"He's been dumpin' all his deliveries on me so he can sit here and spy on you guys," Chase explained.

"What a freak!" Zoey exclaimed.

"I know!" Chase agreed, nodding so emphatically his dark curls bounced. "It's sick," he added distractedly. He was staring at something on the screen. "Oh, hey, there's Quinn." She was center screen, standing next to a large potted plant. Glancing around a little nervously, Quinn bit off a piece of leaf like a jungle animal and started to chew.

"Did she just eat a leaf?" Chase asked in disbelief.

"Stop looking!" Zoey chastised. "It's wrong to spy

on people!" Leaf eating *was* totally weird, but still. Zoey guessed Quinn just couldn't help herself — especially when she knew about the Webcam.

Chase pointed at the computer screen. "But that's a fake plant!" he said.

"Chase!" Zoey blew her bangs out of her eyes, exasperated.

Chase pulled his eyes away from the computer screen. "Right, you gotta get rid of that bear — like, right now."

Zoey tapped a finger on her chin. A fabulous idea was sneaking its way into her head. An idea that involved getting back at Logan. "Or not," she said mischievously.

"Or not?" Chase echoed. He could tell Zoey was up to something.

"Maybe we keep the bear and have a little fun with Logan." Zoey smiled as the idea took shape.

Chase nodded knowingly. "Ahhhh, a little payback."

"Or a lotta payback," Zoey corrected. Logan had crossed the line with the girls, and it was time he realized what a foolish mistake that was. "Come with me."

Chase barely heard her. He was back to staring at the computer screen, and at Quinn, who was still munching away. "She's eating a plastic plant!" he cried, pointing to Quinn.

Zoey rushed back to Chase and grabbed him by the arm. "Come on!" she said. She pulled him away from the computer and out of his room. There was no time to lose.

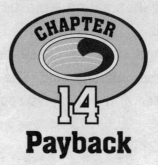

CHAPTER 14
Payback

Zoey stood in one of the PCA courtyards gazing determinedly at the group of girls — and Chase and Michael — in front of her. They'd hatched a plan, and it was almost time to put it into motion.

"Okay, does everyone know the plan?" she asked, looking around at the girls assembled in front of her.

The girls nodded. They'd been furious when Zoey had told them about the Webcam but had quickly turned their anger into determination when Zoey had laid out her plan.

"Good," Chase said. He was second-in-command on this scheme and was taking the job seriously. He didn't want to let the girls — especially Zoey — down. Standing beside him in a flowered peasant skirt and braids, she looked ready for action. Chase wanted to be up to the task, too.

"Remember, everybody be in the girls' lounge at eight-fifteen tonight. I'll show up at around eight-twenty. That's when it all goes down." He nodded seriously.

Dana considered the plan, her arms folded across her chest. She was concerned about one thing. "Wait. How do we know that Logan'll be watching the Webcam?" she asked.

Michael smirked. "Oh, don't worry. We watch every night. Like once"— he pointed to a girl standing behind him —"we saw her dribble spaghetti sauce on her shirt and then she —" He suddenly noticed that twenty girls were glaring at him. And he knew he couldn't blame them, either. "But now I know that's wrong. To spy. On people. Very, very wrong." He held up his hands in mock defense. "I'll make sure he's watching," he finished. It was the least he could do.

"Okay," Zoey piped up. "Let's make sure we have everything we need. She looked down at her checklist on a PCA clipboard.

"Right." Chase took over. "Quinn, you got the cue cards?" he asked.

Quinn held up several cue cards with dialogue written on them. "Got 'em right here," she said.

Zoey nodded. "Nicole, you got the breakaway vase from the drama club?"

Nicole held up a large clear vase. "Breakaway vase — check!" she replied, feeling exhilarated by the plan. Getting back at Logan was going to be fun! As far as she was concerned, he had it coming.

Vicky looked over Nicole's shoulder. "What's a breakaway vase?" she asked.

Nicole smiled sneakily. "Oh, it's fake. You can smash it over someone's head and it doesn't even hurt." She got to her feet and looked around for someone to try it out on. "Check it out," she said, walking up to an unsuspecting janitor.

SMASH! The vase broke into tiny pieces that rained down on the janitor's blue uniform. "See?" Nicole said excitedly as the janitor gave Nicole a look, shook himself off, and kept sweeping.

"Um, Nicole?" Zoey said. The vase was broken now, and they couldn't use it!

Nicole suddenly realized her mistake. "Right," she said, slinking back to her seat, looking sheepish. "I'll get another one."

At exactly eight-fifteen, Michael paced back and forth in his room. He was relieved not to be spying on the girls anymore — as fun as it was, he'd been feeling guilty about it for a while. But he was worried about the plan.

What if it didn't work? Logan was usually back at their dorm by now. Where was he?

His phone rang. Grabbing it out of his pocket, he opened it. "What's up, Chase?" he said nervously.

"Is Logan back yet?" Chase asked on the other end of the line.

"No!" Michael replied, feeling a little panicked. "I don't know where —"

All of a sudden the door opened and Logan strolled into the room, swigging a bottle of water.

"Ummmm, sure!" Michael said into the phone. "I will vote yes on prop forty-six." He flipped his phone closed and shoved it into his pocket.

"Hello," he greeted, smiling at Logan.

"What's up?" Logan asked casually.

"Nothing, nothing." Michael tried to sound nonchalant. "Hey, you know what'd be fun to do right now?" he asked.

Logan shrugged. "What's that?" he asked.

Michael slung an arm around Logan's shoulders and led him toward his desk and computer. "Let's check out the Webcam — see what them girls are up to." He flashed Logan a mischievous smile.

Logan grinned. "I vote yes on that proposition," he said emphatically. He walked over to his desk, pulled out a chair, and sat down. Clicking VIEW on his menu, a new window opened. Hello, girls' lounge!

In the lounge, the girls were pretending to hang out like they normally did. Some watched TV, some worked on laptops, and some chatted. It was a mellow evening scene — until Chase burst into the room, looking nervous.

"Hey, sushi's here!" Zoey said, happily getting to her feet.

The girls surrounded Chase like hungry baby birds. "Thanks, Chase," Nicole said gratefully. "We love the free sushi."

In his dorm room, Logan looked surprised. "Free sushi?" he asked, sitting up a little straighter.

Michael squinted at the screen indignantly. "How come they don't have to pay?"

Logan nodded, ignoring the fact that he had scarfed down plenty of free sushi himself. "They're supposed to," he said indignantly.

"Look, girls," Chase said in the girls' lounge. He was reading the cue cards that Quinn was holding off camera. "I don't know if I can keep hooking you up with all of this free sushi." He gestured to the boxes sitting on the coffee table. "I think my boss is starting to get a little suspicious."

"Kazu?" Zoey asked.

Chase nodded and lowered his voice. "Yeah. So listen, if anybody asks, just say —"

Before he could finish, a furious Kazu stormed into the lounge. Dressed in a purple robe and headband, he grabbed Chase by the shoulders. "Aha!" he bellowed. "I knew it!"

"Kazu!" Chase said, pretending to jump in surprise and fear.

"Uh-oh," Logan said, staring at the screen. He was totally gripped by the scene.

"You've been stealing all my sushi! Giving it to these girls!" Kazu yelled.

"Ummm, uh, no, that's not true!" Chase protested.

"Yes, it is!" Kazu insisted. "I'm going to tell the dean, and then you will be —"

Kazu waited for Quinn to turn to the next cue card. But Quinn was so distracted by the drama they were acting out, she forgot to turn to the next one! "And then you will be —" he repeated loudly.

Everyone stared at Quinn, but she didn't notice.

"Be what?" Logan asked, desperate to know.

Zoey took control. "Quinn, next card!" she whispered.

Quinn nearly dropped the cards when she realized her mistake. But instead she flipped to the next one.

"Expelled!" Kazu finished loudly. "You will be expelled!"

"Expelled?" Chase echoed nervously.

"Expelled?" Logan cried in disbelief.

"You're going to prison!" Kazu shouted, his face turning red.

"No!" Nicole cried. She wasn't actually sure if that was her line, but she couldn't help it. It was all too terrible!

Zoey picked up the breakaway vase, lifted it high, and smashed it over Kazu's head. A split second later, he fell to the floor in a heap.

"D-did you just see that?" Logan asked, gripping Michael's arm.

"Yeah!" Michael replied, trying to sound alarmed. "She knocked the dude out!" He looked at Logan out of the corner of his eye. The plan was working. He was buying it hook, line, and sinker!

"I'm sorry!" Zoey cried, dropping to her knees beside her victim. His face had landed in a pile of sushi. "I panicked."

Chase kneeled beside his fallen boss and checked for vital signs. "He's out cold," he confirmed.

"Oh, no!" Zoey wailed, really getting into it. She wanted to give Logan a good performance. "Now we're all gonna get expelled!"

"This is insane!" Logan exclaimed, literally sitting on the edge of his seat. His friends had knocked out his boss!

"No," Chase said calmly. "Nobody's getting expelled."

"But he'll wake up eventually and tell the dean what happened!" Nicole protested.

"Yes!" Chase paused, waiting for the next cue card. Quinn could be a little slow. "That's why we have to get rid of him!" he said, eyeing the girls around him.

Logan gasped. "Get rid of him?" he echoed. This was like a cop movie!

"This is insane!" Michael agreed.

"Let's put him in the closet," Zoey said, pointing to the storage closet and trying to sound like a real criminal. She was having a blast.

"Right!" Chase agreed. "Then, late tonight, when everybody's asleep, we'll hot-wire his car, put Kazu in the trunk —"

"And drive him to Mexico!" Zoey finished, pointing a determined finger in the air.

"Did she say Mexico?!" Logan could not believe what he was seeing — or hearing.

"*Sí!*" Michael confirmed.

"But what if the dean finds out?" Nicole asked worriedly as she peered at the fallen Kazu.

"She's got a point," Zoey admitted.

"Hey!" Chase said, gesturing with his hands. "He didn't see who hit him!"

"Right!" Zoey agreed. The best part was coming up. "We'll blame it all on . . . on . . ." She searched for the perfect fall guy. "Logan!" she finished.

"Yeah," someone said.

"Right," another girl agreed.

"Yes!" Nicole added. "Logan!"

"Me?!?!" Logan reeled back from his computer as panic rose inside him. He was innocent!

"Okay, we'll blame the whole thing on Logan," Chase repeated for emphasis. "Stealing the sushi, knockin' out Kazu — everything."

"They're gonna blame everything on me!" Logan said in horror. Desperate, he looked to Michael for advice.

"I heard!" Michael said. He'd never seen his roommate freak out like this, and it was nice to see the tables turned.

"Okay, quick!" Zoey instructed. "Let's put Kazu in the closet!"

All the girls agreed.

Logan could feel his heart pounding in his chest. "I gotta do something!" he cried, grabbing Michael by the shoulders.

Michael tried to look sympathetic. He snapped his fingers. "Go get the dean!" he suggested, as if he'd just thought of it.

"Right! I'll go get the dean!" Logan repeated. If Dean Rivers caught them in the act, his name would be cleared for sure. It was the only way!

"You go get 'em, man!" Michael cheered. "You go get 'em, Logan!"

Logan leaped out of his chair and tore out the door. Shaking his head, Michael chuckled to himself. Mission accomplished.

Logan raced across campus to the dean's apartment. He could hear the water running but ignored it and just walked in. Who cared if the dean was taking a shower? Logan's life was in danger!

"Dean Rivers!" Logan cried, bursting into the administrator's bathroom.

The dean shut off the water and peeked out from behind the shower curtain. "Oh! Logan!?" he exclaimed, obviously completely shocked. "What in the world are you doing in my shower —"

"Quick!" Logan interrupted breathlessly. "Put on your robe! Come with me!"

The dean looked dismayed. "But I'm shampooing!" he replied.

"It's an emergency!" Logan insisted, grabbing the dean by the arm.

The dean threw on his maroon terry-cloth robe and followed Logan out the door. A minute later, they were racing across campus toward the girls' dorm. Logan pulled on Dean Rivers's arm. "Hurry!" he cried.

Shampoo dripped onto Dean Rivers's face. He tried to wipe it away, but it was already too late. "I got suds in my eye!" he cried like a little boy.

Logan didn't slow down. There wasn't a second to spare! He burst into the girls' lounge with Dean Rivers in tow.

"There!" he shouted, pointing to the girls hanging out on the sofas and chairs. "There they are!"

Zoey looked at Logan as if he was the last person she expected to see in the girls' lounge.

"Logan?" Dana said, trying not to smirk. Pulling one over on him was the most fun she'd had all year at PCA.

"Dean Rivers?" Nicole added, looking completely surprised, while inside she was doing a little cheer.

"What's up?" Zoey said, looking up from her knitting.

"You know what's up!" Logan protested. "You've been stealing sushi from Kazu, and when he found out, you knocked him in the head with a vase and shoved him in the closet!" He opened the closet with a flourish, but there was no Kazu inside. It was full of cleaning supplies.

"A vacuum," Dean Rivers said, his hair still full of shampoo. He looked totally peeved.

"You wanna borrow it?" Zoey offered. She almost felt sorry for Logan, but not quite. The little creep deserved everything he got!

Logan would not be defeated so easily. He had seen the whole thing! But where was Kazu?

"I know!" Logan said, snapping his fingers. "They probably already put Kazu in his car."

"What!?" Now Dean Rivers looked concerned and annoyed.

The girls stared at Logan as if he had smoke coming out of his ears. And a second later, Kazu walked into the lounge. Chase was right behind him wearing his Sushi Rox hat.

"Hello, children!" Kazu said cheerfully.

"Kazzzuuuuu!" the girls replied in unison, smiling broadly.

"How's it going, Kazu?" Zoey asked casually.

Logan stared at Kazu as if he were a ghost. "Kazu?" he mumbled.

"Hey, whassup, Logan?" Chase greeted him.

"Oh, hello, Dean Rivers," Kazu said, as if he were seeing the dean for the first time.

"What brings you here, Kazu?" Nicole asked innocently.

"Oh, I was just helping Chase with his deliveries, since Logan is sick." He eyed Logan disdainfully. "But you don't look sick to me," he added.

"He's not sick," Zoey confirmed with a satisfied smile.

Logan was totally embarrassed. And he had to think fast! "Uhh, Kazu, I can explain," he mumbled.

"So can I," Kazu interrupted, with a smirk. "You're fired!" He looked around at the girls in the lounge. "I feel like Donald Trump," he admitted.

"But you got whacked with a vase!" Logan protested. He'd seen it himself on his computer! What was going on?

"What?!" Kazu pointed to himself in surprise.

Dean Rivers stared hard at Logan.

"It's true!" Logan insisted. He couldn't be wrong, could he?

"All right, Mr. Reese. I think your little joke has gone far enough," Dean Rivers said. He was obviously getting a little tired of standing around with shampoo in his hair.

"It's not a joke! I swear!" Logan cried. "I saw everything. See?" He dragged the dean over to the teddy bear in the corner. "I put a Webcam in this teddy bear!"

The girls all pretended to gasp at once. "Logan, I am shocked," Zoey exclaimed, looking thoroughly surprised.

"I'm dismayed," Nicole added.

"Horrified," Dana finished.

"Do you mean to tell me you put a camera in the girls' lounge and you've been spying on them?" Dean Rivers asked angrily.

Logan suddenly felt a little warm. Everyone in the room was staring at him.

"Well . . . yeah, but —"

Dean Rivers had had enough. "All right, mister," he said. "It's time you and I had a little conference call with your parents." He looked apologetically at the girls. "Sorry to interrupt your evening, girls," he said.

The girls nodded understandingly.

"But Dean Rivers!" Logan was still protesting loudly.

"You interrupted my shampoo for nothing!" the dean said hotly, pulling Logan out of the lounge.

As soon as they were gone, the girls erupted into cheers and laughter. Payback had been a success, and revenge was sweet!

"Okay, who wants sushi?" Kazu asked, slapping hands with Chase. It was time to celebrate with some California rolls and sashimi!

A few days later, Zoey, Dana, and Nicole were all sitting together on the sofa in their room looking at Zoey's computer.

"How beautiful is that?" Zoey asked, pointing to the screen with a satisfied smile.

"Gorgeous," Nicole agreed.

Dana nodded. She had to admit it. "Pretty nice."

Just then there was a knock on the door, and Chase appeared in his delivery outfit carrying a sushi tray.

"Somebody order some California rolls?" he asked, flashing them the tray.

"Yep," Zoey replied with a grin. "Hey, you wanna come watch the sunset on the beach?" Zoey asked.

Chase shook his head. "I'm workin'," he said dejectedly. "I can't go to the beach."

"You don't have to," Nicole pointed out with a smile.

"C'mere," Zoey said.

Chase crossed the room, sat down on the couch, and looked at Zoey's computer screen. It showed a beautiful golden-orange sunset over the tranquil Pacific Ocean.

"Wow, niiice," Chase said. Then he looked confused. "But how are you seeing this?"

Zoey smiled slyly, and Chase got the message. Logan's big teddy bear had found a new home — a lounge chair right on the dunes. And spying on the Pacific was something they could *all* appreciate. Maybe someday the girls would even share a sunset with Logan.

Check out these great Teenick Titles!

Girls Got Game
Dramarama
Pranks for Nothing!

Keepin' It Real
Split Ends
Star Struck